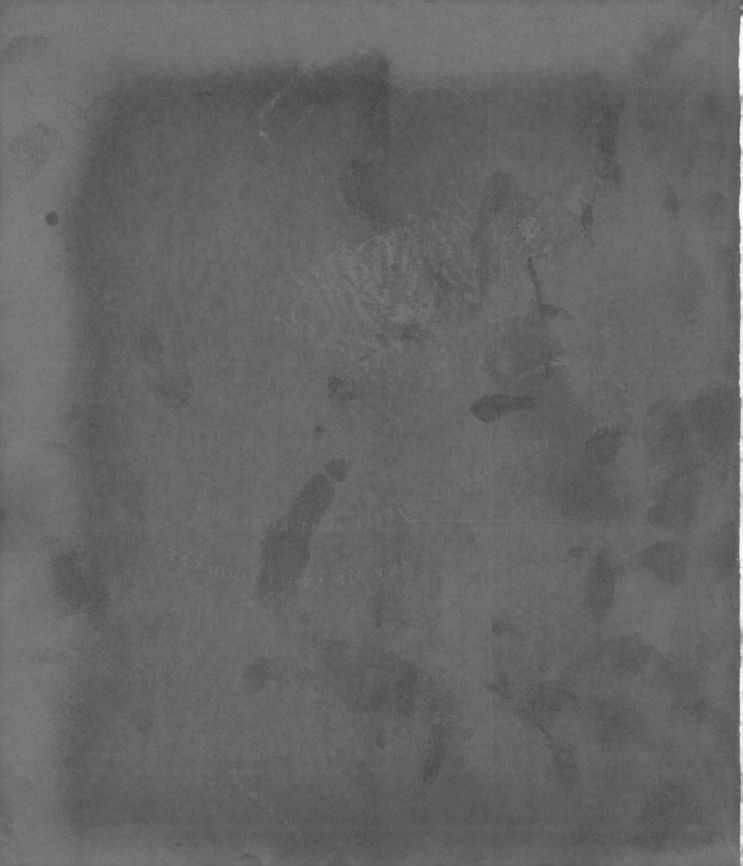

THE HIGH RISE GLORIOUS SKITTLE SKAT ROARIOUS

SKY PIE ANGEL FOOD CAKE

by Nancy Willard

Illustrated by Richard Jesse Watson

THE HIGH RISE GLORIOUS SKITTLE SKAT ROARIOUS SKY PIE ANGEL FOOD CAKE

Lester & Orpen Dennys Limited
Toronto, Canada

FIRST EDITION

Part of a poem by Emily Dickinson is quoted on page 21.
The last two lines of stanza four, taken from poem #737,
are reprinted by permission of the publisher and the Trustees of
Amherst College from The Poems of Emily Dickinson,
Thomas H. Johnson, ed., Cambridge, Mass.:
The Belknap Bress of Harvard University Press,
Copyright 1951, © 1955, 1979, 1983 by the President
and Fellows of Harvard College.

CANADIAN CATALOGUING IN PUBLICATION DATA

    Willard, Nancy
        The high rise glorious skittle skat roarious
    sky high angelfood cake

ISBN 0-88619-294-3

I. Watson, RIchard Jesse. II. Title.

PZ7.W6553Hi 1990   j813'.54   C90-094284-3

Printed and bound for

Lester & Orpen Dennys Limited
78 Sullivan Street,
Toronto, Ontario
M5T 1C1

For Bonnie, the guardian angel
of this enterprise   — N. W.

For Faithy   — R. J. W.

Angels fly because they take themselves lightly.
—G. K. CHESTERTON

THE HIGH RISE GLORIOUS SKITTLE SKAT ROARIOUS

SKY PIE ANGEL FOOD CAKE

*L*et me tell you
about my angels.

But first, let me tell you about my dad. Three days before my mom's birthday, Dad took me aside and asked, "Can you find out what your mother wants? When I ask her, she says, 'Oh, don't spend a lot of money on me. I already have everything I want.'"

"Maybe she *does* have everything she wants," I said.

"No," said Dad. "Everybody wants something."

Last year he bought her a dress that didn't fit. The year before he bought her a big red purse, and she took it back to the store and traded it for a teeny green one. The year before that he bought her a teapot shaped like a cat, and when she filled it with tea the bottom dropped out. I know Dad does the best he can, but Mom deserves better.

"Okay," I said. "I'll ask her what she wants."

Mom was kneeling in the backyard, digging up dandelions and talking out of the side of her mouth to the rosebushes. Let me tell you about my mom. She says if you talk to your flowers, they'll grow better. Spring and summer I hear her asking the roses if they need anything. More water, more fertilizer? Once she heard a dandelion trying to roar. She said it sounded like a grasshopper yawning.

"Mom," I said, "what do you want for your birthday?"

"Make me something," she answered. "I like the presents you make best of all."

"Okay," I said. "What do you want me to make?"

"A birthday cake," said Mom. "You could make me a birthday cake."

"Okay," I said. "What kind of cake do you like?"

"Chocolate," said Mom. "You love chocolate."

"But this cake is for you," I said. "What kind of cake do *you* like?"

She didn't answer for a long time. She just kept digging out dandelions. And when she finally spoke, her voice seemed to come far from this time and place.

"When I was seven years old, my grandmother made me the most wonderful birthday cake. Oh, I've never forgotten it. She called it a High Rise Glorious Skittle Skat Roarious Sky Pie Angel Food Cake."

"Is it in *The Joy of Cooking?*" I asked. Out of the corner of my eye I saw Dad hovering by the front door, trying to eavesdrop on us.

"No," answered my mother. "It's not in any cookbook. When I asked my grandmother for the recipe, she said it was just like the recipe for ordinary angel food cake except for one secret ingredient."

"What was that?"

"She wouldn't tell me. She said I'd have to find out for myself."

"And did you?"

"No. And now she's dead and gone to heaven. But I'll never forget that High Rise Glorious Skittle Skat Roarious Sky Pie Angel Food Cake as long as I live. She baked a golden thimble into the cake, and she said whoever got it would be lucky for a year."

"Who got it?"

"She got it herself."

Dad met me halfway down the front steps.

"Well? What did your mom say?"

"She wants a High Rise Glorious Skittle Skat Roarious Sky Pie Angel Food Cake."

"A cake? She wants a cake? She never eats cake. She's always dieting."

"I'm just telling you what she told me."

"Tell me again."

"She wants a High Rise Glorious Skittle Skat Roarious Sky Pie Angel Food Cake."

Dad whipped out his *Daily Reminder* notepad and scribbled down the name. Then he tucked the notepad into his shirt pocket and smiled at me.

"Thank heaven that problem's settled. I'll call Capital Bakery and put in an order."

"You can't order this cake," I said, "and it's not in any cookbook. And it's made with a secret ingredient. And only my great-grandmother knew the secret."

Dad threw up his hands and went off to buy Mom a bathrobe.

Let me tell you about my great-grandmother. She had a grand piano and a house full of books. She loved to play the grand piano and read. Sometimes she did both at the same time. Whenever my great-grandmother ran across some interesting item she wanted to remember, she copied it into a leather-bound notebook. She filled thirty-two leather-bound notebooks, all titled "Ledger" and numbered like an encyclopedia. When she died, she willed me her grand piano, which I can have when I grow up, and her thirty-two notebooks, which I can have any time I want them. For a long time I didn't want them. But I couldn't throw away a gift from my great-grandmother. So I put them in the Big Box of Dreadfuls in the cellar.

Let me tell you about that box. The Big Box of Dreadfuls is full of stuff we don't want but we're afraid to throw away. There's a hideous ceramic vase in the shape of a football that Uncle Harry and Aunt Carolyn gave Mom and Dad for a wedding present, and a self-portrait painted by Aunt Carolyn, who didn't think the vase was grand enough.

The self-portrait shows her as a young girl, petting a bald dog and sitting by a waterfall, which she will never do again, because last year she and Uncle Harry took a bus to Niagara Falls, and Aunt Carolyn dropped her purse over the edge. Pouf! A hundred dollars flushed out of sight. When Uncle Harry and Aunt Carolyn call on us, Mom puts the vase on the mantel and hangs the self-portrait over the grand piano. After they leave, she packs them both away in the Box of Dreadfuls.

At the bottom of the Box of Dreadfuls lay my great-grandmother's thirty-two leather-bound notebooks. I lugged them upstairs to bed with me, and after my mother went downstairs, I pulled out my flashlight and started to read them.

The first seven notebooks were full of poems and little slips of helpful sayings like "Grief in the evening is joy in the morning." The poems mostly talked about love. A few talked about God. The one I liked best didn't talk about anything. It just painted a picture of the moon.

The moon was but a chin of gold
    A night or two ago,
And now she turns her perfect face
    Upon the world below.

And what a privilege to be
    But the remotest star!
For certainly her way might pass
    Beside your twinkling door.

After she'd filled the seventh notebook, my great-grandmother gave up poetry and turned to crime. In notebooks eight through fifteen she'd pasted stories from the newspaper about interesting murders and thefts. A burglar in Norfolk, Connecticut, stole a case of hot dogs from a nursing home and was found the next morning asleep in front of the icebox. A florist in Kansas City, Missouri, tried to murder his partner's ghost and died of fright. A schoolteacher who discovered she could be in two places at once robbed a bank in Toledo while her better half was teaching algebra to tenth-graders in Cleveland. I forgot all about the High Rise Glorious Skittle Skat Roarious Sky Pie Angel Food Cake until I picked up notebook sixteen. It was titled "Recipes." All the recipes had names that sounded as if my great-grandmother had invented them:

First National Bank

Stout Cake

Delicate Cake

Drop Cake

Plain Cake

Lady Baltimore Cake

Porcupine Icebox Cake

Pyramid Cake

Quick Cake

Cheap Cake

Imperial Sunshine Cake

On the second-to-the-last page, I found:

Angel Food Cake, Ordinary.

$1\frac{1}{2}$ *cups egg-whites, 12 or 13*

$1\frac{1}{4}$ *teaspoons cream of tartar*

$\frac{1}{2}$ *teaspoon salt*

$1\frac{1}{2}$ *cups granulated sugar measured lightly*

1 cup plus 2 tablespoons cake flour

Beat egg-whites, add cream of tartar and salt when eggs are frothy. Continue beating till a point of the egg-whites will stand upright. Fold in the flour and the sugar and pour into ungreased tube pan and bake for one hour at 325° F.

My heart stopped for a second. Below the recipe my great-grandmother had written, in tiny letters,

"TODAY I INVENTED THE RECIPE FOR THE HIGH RISE GLORIOUS SKITTLE SKAT ROARIOUS SKY PIE ANGEL FOOD CAKE. BUT IT'S TOO DANGEROUS. IT IS IRRESISTIBLE TO MAN AND BEAST, WOMAN AND BIRD. I FEAR IT MAY FALL INTO THE WRONG HANDS. SO I'VE NOTED IN A DARK PLACE THE RECIPE, WHICH I COMPOSED MYSELF, AFTER PLAYING AROUND IN THE KITCHEN."

Well, that depressed me. To have almost found it was worse than not finding it at all. But I told myself not to worry. Rising early clears the brain. I turned out my flashlight, tucked the notebook under my pillow, and fell asleep. And who did I see in my sleep but my great-grandmother playing the grand piano and singing,

Right at hand or left at foot?
Who will help the helpless cook?

"Great-Grandmother!" I called. "Tell me the secret!"

She waved at me and shook her head, and the piano tried to escape with her into the air.

"Please, please!" I shouted and plunged after them and hit my head on the keyboard cover. Great-Grandmother stopped singing, and the piano howled, and I woke up. Right below my room, Mom was vacuuming.

I jumped out of bed, pulled on my jeans and T-shirt, and ran downstairs. Right away I noticed Aunt Carolyn's painting over the piano and

Uncle Harry's ceramic football on the mantel. Oh, let me tell you about my uncle. He's my mom's brother, and he always spills things when he visits us. Usually it's coffee on the paisley tablecloth in the kitchen, but last Thanksgiving he upset a whole pitcher of gravy on the rug. "No harm done," said Uncle Harry.

"He was always like that," groaned Mom in my ear. "Bring the baking soda." The rug in our dining room has lots of pale, thin spots where she's rubbed it with baking soda.

When she saw me, Mom switched off the vacuum.

"Uncle Harry and Aunt Carolyn are coming today," she said.

"For lunch?"

"No, just for dessert. We'll eat in the living room."

Uncle Harry had ruined so many tablecloths I guess Mom figured she'd keep him out of the dining room for the rest of his life. But at least she'd forgiven him. When I opened the refrigerator, I saw she'd made his favorite red Jell-O salad, molded in little dishes shaped like stars. She knew how much Uncle Harry loved that salad.

An hour later, Dad and Mom and I and Uncle Harry and Aunt Carolyn were all gathered in the living room. And Mom said to me, "Will you serve the salad?"

I brought in the tray and passed it, and everybody took a Jell-O star and a spoon. My uncle was eating his star in an absentminded sort of way and admiring the ceramic football on the mantel.

"I'm glad to see you get so much use out of that vase," said Uncle Harry.

"Yup," said my dad.

Aunt Carolyn was squinting at her painting over the piano.

"It's hung crooked," she said.

My uncle sprang up. He held his Jell-O in his left hand and adjusted the picture with his right.

"Tip it a little more to your side," said Aunt Carolyn.

He pulled it toward himself.

"No, a little more to the left."

He tipped it the other way.

"I think it looked fine where it was," said my dad.

"I've noticed," said Aunt Carolyn, "that a lot of people keep pictures on the piano."

My uncle yanked the picture off the wall and tried setting it on the piano. This way, that way. Then something behind the picture caught his eye.

"Wow," he said. "Just look at all those strings."

"What strings?" asked Mom.

"You can see inside the whole piano. Stand right here."

And he waved his left hand. His Jell-O hand. The whole thing slithered out of the dish straight down into the piano. Plip-plop!

"Oh, I'm sorry," cried my uncle.

"It's nothing," whispered Mother. She looked wild.

"I'll get the baking soda," I told her, but she shook her head.

"No; bring a dry dishtowel. And a flashlight."

When I arrived with the towel and the light, my aunt sat at the piano and tried a few chords. The piano made a damp, embarrassed noise.

"Let me help," said my uncle and took the light from me. He leaned over the piano and shone the light across the hammers and strings. Then he looked up and smiled.

"Why, there's no harm done. The Jell-O has disappeared."

"Disappeared!" cried my mom.

Dad turned to me.

"*You* take a look," he said. "You have the best eyes here."

I shone the light all around inside the piano. Strings. Hammers. No Jell-O. I figured the piano ate it. Why shouldn't a piano like Jell-O?

"I hope it didn't drip through," said Mom.

I scrunched down and turned the beam on the underside of the piano. No Jell-O. But there, in my great-grandmother's spidery hand, I saw the words:

HIGH RISE GLORIOUS SKITTLE SKAT ROARIOUS
SKY PIE ANGEL FOOD CAKE.

Make just like regular angel food and use secret ingredient: Before adding sugar, sprinkle it out on a plate and write with the first finger of your left hand:

EVOL-EVOL-EVOL.

After dinner I gathered all my ingredients — eggs, cream of tartar, salt, sugar, and flour — while I was supposed to be washing the supper dishes, and I hid them in the back of the refrigerator. I found the mixing bowl and the electric beater and the measuring cup and spoons and the round tube pan with the hole in the middle. I pushed them into the space under the sink. Also, Mom's best cake plate, with pansies painted on it. But I didn't have a golden thimble. I'd never even seen a *golden* thimble.

I decided to set my alarm clock for midnight. That way I'd have the kitchen to myself, unless my dad fell asleep on the sofa watching a basketball game, which he occasionally does on weekends.

Five minutes before midnight I sat up in bed, wide awake, and nipped the alarm in the bud. I climbed out of bed and tiptoed past the door of my parents' room. The way my dad snores would scare a lot of people who didn't know him. For Valentine's Day my mom bought him a chin strap and a pillow with a hole in the middle. The ad on TV said these remedies had been tested on an Alaskan moose with a similar problem. On Mother's Day my mom received an anonymous gift of earplugs. She thought I sent them to her, but I didn't.

Not a stair creaked when I crept down to the kitchen.

Full moon! I didn't even need to turn on the light.

I lugged out the mixing bowl and my ingredients. I cracked twelve eggs — the whole box — and slid the whites very carefully into the bowl. Dad likes an egg for breakfast, but I was sure that he'd gladly do without for so worthy a cause. The egg-whites took forever to turn frothy, and I had to hold a towel over the beater to keep it quiet.

Egg-whites. Salt. Cream of tartar, which looks like powdered sugar and tastes so bad I don't know why my great-grandmother included it. Flour.

Last of all, I rolled the sugar out on the breadboard and wrote with the first finger of my left hand:

EVOL-EVOL-EVOL.

Nothing happened. Suddenly I felt stupid. What did I expect? I stirred in the sugar, poured the batter into the tube pan, turned the oven to 325 degrees, and popped the cake inside.

And then I sat down on the little stepstool to wait. Too bad I didn't bring my flashlight and a magazine, I thought. I crept into the living room and brought back a sofa pillow and the afghan and curled up on the floor opposite the oven.

The kitchen felt stuffy and hot. Heaven forbid I should fall asleep at such an important moment! I opened the window and drew my pillow and afghan near it. The cold air would keep me awake. In one hour I would check on the cake.

I closed my eyes — they felt heavy, but I didn't fall asleep. I'm pretty sure of that. A rustling in the kitchen startled me. I dislike mice except in cages, and I opened my eyes in a hurry.

The oven door hung open. Three angels were peering into it. Their robes swept the linoleum floor, and their wings and halos glimmered in the friendly light of the full moon. Hearing me, they turned. The halo of the biggest angel brushed the cobwebs on the ceiling.

"Good evening," said the biggest angel.

"Good evening," said I, catching my breath.

"That's a fine cake you've made," said the middle angel.

"I think so myself," I said. My voice sounded pinched, as if it were coming out of a bottle. The smallest angel gave me a sweet smile. All at once I felt I'd known them all my life.

"It's been a long time since we've tasted a cake made at the hands of a mortal child," said the biggest angel.

"A long time," said the middle one. "In heaven, the Welcome Cakes are made by angels. But I believe yours smells sweeter."

I could hardly believe my ears.

"You smelled my cake in heaven?"

The angels nodded.

"Irresistible," said the smallest angel.

"Divine," added the middle angel.

"In heaven, when people arrive after a long journey," said the biggest angel, "they're invited to sit at the heavenly table."

I stole a glance at our tablecloth. It was stained, where Uncle Harry spilled the coffee. But could I refuse an angel?

"Please sit down," I said.

The angels drew up four chairs.

"We couldn't enjoy ourselves if you weren't sitting with us," said the smallest angel.

"What a beautiful tablecloth," said the biggest angel. "Why, it has Brother Bear painted on it!"

The moment he said it, the coffee stain looked exactly like a brown bear running through the paisleys. I hadn't noticed it before.

"You'll want to check on your cake, I suppose," said the middle angel, "to see if it's done."

I jumped up, pulled a straw from the broom in the corner, opened the oven door, and poked the cake, the way I've seen my mom do, to see if the cake was done.

"You'll want potholders to take it out, I suppose," said the middle angel, "so you don't burn yourself."

I put on Mom's potholder gloves and lifted the cake out. The angels leaned forward as I turned the pan upside down on the pansy plate.

"Can we see the cake?" asked the smallest angel.

"If I take it out before it's cool, it'll fall apart," I explained.

"I believe it's cool right now," said the middle angel. "Try it."

I picked up the pan and shook it. To my astonishment, the cake dropped out, perfectly round on all sides. A golden ring.

"In heaven," said the biggest angel, "when people sit at the heavenly table, they're invited to eat of the Welcome Cake."

My heart sank. A cake with three pieces missing — what kind of present is that? If I cut the pieces thin, I could close the ring up. An oval cake tastes just as good as a round one.

So I brought three napkins and three forks and a knife, and I cut the first piece. A mere sliver. I was about to cut the second when the biggest angel said, "In heaven, when people are invited to eat of the Welcome Cake at the heavenly table, they are given a big piece."

I blushed and edged the knife over a little more.

"Sometimes," said the middle angel, "we even let them cut their own."

I was going to say, If I let you cut your own, there'll hardly be any-thing left for Mom and Dad and me. Then I thought, Can I be stingy with angels? I'll have time to make another cake before morning.

Oh, they would see how generous I could be! I cut the entire cake into three pieces, and eased the pieces onto the napkins and handed them around. The angels fanned their wings with pleasure.

Each angel broke a piece in two and handed it to me.

"We couldn't enjoy this cake if you weren't enjoying it, too," said the smallest angel.

As the angels were nibbling the crumbs, I thought of something so terrible that I choked on my last bite.

"What's the matter?" asked the middle angel.

"I just remembered I used up all the eggs. I can't bake my mother another cake."

"Your mother?" exclaimed the biggest angel. "You made this cake for your mother?"

"Tomorrow is her birthday. All she wanted for her birthday was a High Rise Glorious Skittle Skat Roarious Sky Pie Angel Food Cake." In spite of myself, I burst into tears. "She's such a *nice* mother," I roared. "And it was such a beautiful cake!"

The three angels looked at each other.

"Close your eyes," said the biggest angel. "Whatever you hear, whatever you smell, don't open your eyes. And don't speak."

I closed my eyes. Around me, their robes swished across the floor and their wings beat the air. My great-grandmother's saying sang in my ears: *Grief in the evening is joy in the morning.* Suddenly a tremendous clatter of pots and pans nearly knocked me out of my chair. That does it, I thought. Mom and Dad will be down in two minutes.

But they did not come down. Such a long silence followed that I felt sure the angels must have left. As I was about to open my eyes, I heard whispering.

"Everything is different down here. We'll have to go for help."

Heaven forbid that I should open my eyes at such an important moment. I sat so still that both my legs went numb. A breeze from the open window chilled me.

And now an emptiness settled over the kitchen: the silence left by angels that have vanished. I opened my eyes. Did I doze off? The kitchen was cleaned up, everything put away. Deep disappointment settled over me like a black cloud.

There was no cake on the table. Even the plate was gone.

Mom's best plate with the pansies, I thought. You can't trust anyone these days.

It was too early to stay up. I marched back to bed, but I didn't fall asleep. No, I lay awake for hours and then listened to the sounds of Mom and Dad rising. Voices, laughter, Dad's loose change tinkling off the bureau to the floor. Grief knotted itself at the bottom of my stomach when Mom poked her head in my room and said, "Let's all have breakfast together. I'm going to open my presents."

Mom and I sat at the dining room table in state and glory. Dad was in the kitchen scraping the toast, which he had burned, but so what? At her plate he'd left a large box from Jacobson's, wrapped in gold paper.

"Come join us," my mom called to him.

Dad pulled up his chair, and his eyes danced as she ran her fingernail along the Scotch tape and pulled the paper off in one piece and folded it.

She lifted the top of the box. Under a thin layer of tissue lay a white terrycloth robe, thick and soft as a cloud.

"Oh, I've always wanted a terrycloth robe!"

She hugged Dad. She hugged the robe. She tried it on. A perfect fit. I knew she wouldn't exchange this present. Of all the clothes she owned, this robe would be her favorite. She'd wear it to pieces. Dad was grinning from ear to ear. Finally he'd given her something she really wanted.

Now it was my turn. I knew they were waiting.

"My present — I have to make it over again," I explained. "It will be a little late."

I felt just awful. Giving someone a birthday cake the day after her birthday is like putting up a Christmas tree the day after Christmas.

"Better late than never," said my father.

"I love late presents," said Mom. "They make the fun last longer."

Mom had a knack for making the best of a bad deal. She noticed that Dad had forgotten to pour the orange juice, so she put on her new robe and padded barefoot into the kitchen, humming.

"Did you make toast in the oven?" she called to Dad.

"No," he answered.

"That's strange. The oven is on."

I ran into the kitchen. Dad followed. I laid my hand on the oven. It was cold. I'm very careful about turning off electrical things. But a golden light was streaming around the door, as if something inside wanted our attention.

Mom opened the door and gave a cry of astonishment.

"What a beautiful cake! And all frosted — how on earth did you make it?"

"Surprise," I said. Nobody was more surprised than I.

"Never mind the toast," said Mom. "Let's have cake for breakfast."

She carried the cake high over her head and set it right in the middle of the table. The golden crust didn't show under the sugar roses and the sugar hearts.

"It's almost too beautiful to eat," said Mom.

Since we were all hungry, she cut three pieces. I was dying to taste mine, but Dad said, "Your mom should take the first bite."

Mom bit into the cake. She closed her eyes. And in a voice that seemed to come far from this time and place she whispered, "High Rise Glorious Skittle Skat Roarious Sky Pie Angel Food Cake. This is the real thing. Just the way my grandmother made it."

Dad bit into his piece.

"Heavenly," he said. Now he was the one looking surprised.

Suddenly Mom stopped eating. Her teeth crunched down on something hard. She spit it out — was it a button? — into her hand and turned it this way, that way.

"A golden thimble!" she exclaimed. "Where on earth did you find a golden thimble?"

"That's my secret." I smiled. Not because I wouldn't tell her, but because I didn't know.

The illustrations in this book were done in egg tempera on Masonite.
The text type was set in Garamond #3 by Thompson Type, San Diego, California.
The display type was handlettered by Judythe Sieck.
The color separation for the jacket was made by Colorscan Systems, San Diego, California.
The color separations for the text were made by Bright Arts, Ltd., Singapore.
Printed and bound by Tien Wah Press, Singapore
Production supervision by Warren Wallerstein and Michele Green
Designed by Joy Chu

Special thanks to Barry Moser